Karen's Big Joke

**Look for these
and other books about Karen
in the
Baby-sitters Little Sister series:**

Little Sister

Karen's Big Joke

Ann M. Martin

Illustrations by Susan Tang

AN
APPLE
PAPERBACK

SCHOLASTIC INC.
New York Toronto London Auckland Sydney

ISBN 0-590-44829-3

12 11 10 9 8 7 6 5 4 3   3 4 5 6 7/9

Printed in the U.S.A.   40

First Scholastic printing, April 1992

For Elisa Geliebter,
with thanks

McBuzz's Mail Order

Hello. My name is Karen Brewer and I just love holidays. I love any special day. I love my birthday and Thanksgiving and Halloween. And I love little holidays like May Day and April Fools' Day. Right now I am excited because April Fools' Day is coming. I cannot wait to say, "April Fool!" when I play jokes on my friends and the people in my two families.

I am in second grade and I have a very wonderful teacher. Her name is Ms. Colman. Ms. Colman likes holidays, too. She told us some things about April Fools' Day. She said that people in many countries celebrate the day, but no one is sure how April Fooling first began. One April Fool story is about a king who lived a long, *long*, LONG time ago. King John was angry at the people in a little town in England. So he sent one of his officers to punish them. But the people found out about his visit. When the officer arrived, the people were doing silly things, such as rolling cheeses down hills. The officer thought the people were fools, so King John decided not to waste time punishing them. Maybe King John was the first April Fool!

Today, everyone likes to play tricks and jokes on April Fools' Day. These are some good jokes: Put salt in the sugar bowl. Send someone on a silly errand. Hide a rubber spider under your sister's pillow. *But . . .* Ms. Colman says always remember that April Fooling is supposed to be fun. You are not supposed to play tricks that are too mean or scary. And of course, you should never play a trick that could hurt someone.

I could think of lots of April Fools' Day tricks to play. So could my second-grade friends. And so could my brothers and sisters. McBuzz's Mail Order is a catalog. It is just full of gigundoly wonderful tricks you can order. The people at McBuzz's mail your tricks to you. (That is why the catalog is called McBuzz's *Mail Order*.) I had spent a lot of time turning the pages of the catalog. My little brother, Andrew, had done the same thing.

"Look, Karen!" Andrew would say. "There is a fake ice cube with a fly in it. If you put it in someone's drink, he will think a fly got in the ice cube tray! He will say, 'Ew, ew!' and then you will say — "

"April Fool!" I supplied. "And look. Here is trick soap. When someone washes with it, his hands turn blue!"

Andrew giggled. Then he pointed to another picture in the catalog. "What is that?" he asked. (Andrew is only four. He cannot read yet.)

"It is a squirting camera," I told him. "See? You hold it up to someone and you say, 'Cheese!' and when the person stops and smiles, you press the button, and the camera squirts water in his face!"

"Cool!" cried my brother. "I want to order that."

I wanted the camera, too. Plus, I wanted this very gross plastic bug. The bug was huge. It was called a cockroach. It would be good for hiding, like in the soap dish or maybe in someone's shoe.

Andrew and I asked Mommy if we could each order three tricks for April Fools' Day. Mommy said yes. I decided to order the cockroach and the trick soap and also some trick gum that would taste like pepper. Andrew decided to order the fly in the ice cube and a rubber spider and the squirting camera. He promised to share the camera with me.

"Thank you, Andrew," I said. "We will be able to squirt lots of people on April Fools' Day this year. That is because we will be at the big house on April Fools' Day. I already checked the calendar."

Cartwheels

Maybe you are wondering what the big house is. The big house is my daddy's house. My mommy lives in another house, a little one. My mommy and daddy are divorced. That is why they live in different houses. It is also why I have two families.

Here is what happened. A long time ago, Mommy and Daddy got married. They had two children — Andrew and me — and we all lived in the big house. (Daddy grew up in that house.) After awhile, my parents decided they did not want to live together anymore. They did not love each other. They loved Andrew and me but not each other. So Mommy moved out of the big house. She took Andrew and me with her. She moved into a little house. The little house is not too far from Daddy's. Both houses are in Stoneybrook, Connecticut.

Pretty soon, Mommy and Daddy got married again, but not to each other. Mommy married Seth Engle. Seth is my stepfather. He moved into the little house with us. And he brought along his cat, Rocky, and his dog, Midgie. Now they live with Mommy and Andrew and Seth and me. Oh, and with Emily Junior. Emily Junior is my rat.

Mommy's house is a quiet place.

Daddy married Elizabeth Thomas. Now Elizabeth is my stepmother. She moved into the big house. And she brought along her four children. Daddy's house is noisy and busy! Elizabeth's sons are Charlie, Sam, and David Michael. They are my stepbrothers. Charlie and Sam are in high school. David Michael is seven like me, but he goes to a different school. Elizabeth's daughter is Kristy, my stepsister. Kristy is thirteen and she baby-sits. I *love* Kristy. Also, I am glad to have a sister.

Wait. *More* people live at the big house. One of them is Emily Michelle. She is two and a half, and she is my adopted sister. Daddy and Elizabeth adopted her from a country called Vietnam. Vietnam is far, far away. Another person is Nannie. She is Elizabeth's mother, so she is my stepgrandmother. Nannie moved in to help take care of Emily. (By the way, I named my rat after Emily.)

Plus, some pets live at Daddy's. Shannon is David Michael's puppy. Boo-Boo is Daddy's old, cross cat. And Goldfishie and Crystal Light the Second are the fish that belong to Andrew and me.

Andrew and I live mostly at the little house and partly at the big house. We live at the big house every other weekend and on some holidays and vacations. In between we live with Mommy and Seth. Can you guess why I call my brother and me Andrew Two-Two and Karen Two-Two? It is because we have two of so many things. (I got the name from a book Ms. Colman read to our class. It was called *Jacob Two-Two Meets the Hooded Fang*.) Andrew and I have two houses and two families, two mommies and two daddies, two cats and two dogs. I have two bicycles, one at each house. I have two stuffed cats. Moosie lives at the big house, Goosie lives at the little house. Plus, I have clothes and books and toys at each house. I even have two best friends. Nancy Dawes is my little-house best friend. She lives next door to Mommy. Hannie Papadakis is my big-house best friend. She lives across the street from Daddy and one house down. Nancy and Hannie are in Ms. Colman's class, too. We call ourselves the Three Musketeers.

My life is quite busy. I go to school. I play with my friends. I travel back and forth between Mommy's house and Daddy's house. I write letters to Maxie. Maxie is my pen pal in New York City. Also, I take gymnastics. I have been taking gymnastics for awhile now. I finished the first beginners class. Now I am waiting for the second beginners class to start. I can do a forward roll and a backward roll. *But* — I cannot turn a cartwheel. Yet.

Oh, well. A busy two-two cannot do everything.

Old Friends, New Friends

"Mommy, my feet smell."

"Karen."

"Well, they do." I was sitting on the floor at my gymnastics school. I was wearing my purple leotard and my pink leggings. And I was holding one of my feet up to my nose. I breathed in. "Oh, pew," I said.

"Honey, really," said Mommy. "Is that necessary? Anyway, please do not worry about your feet. If they smell it is because you just took off your sneakers. You were running around in gym today."

"Yeah. Let your feet air out a little," said Andrew.

"Mommy, does he have to be here?" I asked. I pointed to my brother.

"I don't know what else to do with him," said Mommy.

"Maybe you could leave now," I suggested.

"I want to make sure you find your new class," Mommy answered. "Then Andrew and I will leave."

We waited in the hallway at gymnastics school. We waited until I saw my teacher. "Hi, Miss Donovan!" I called. "Mommy, there is Miss Donovan. Now you can leave."

I followed Miss Donovan into one of the practice rooms. I could not wait to see the kids in my gymnastics class again. Here is who was in my first beginners class: Maria, Dana, Kitty, Scott, Taisa, Robbie, and me. We had so much fun together.

I stood by the doorway and waited for Dana. But the first person who came into

12

the room was a girl I had not seen before. Hmm. A new student. Well, Dana and I would introduce her to the kids in the class.

The next person who arrived was *another* new kid.

The next person was Jannie Gilbert. Jannie is in my class at school. But I had not seen her at gymnastics before.

"What are you doing here?" I asked Jannie.

"Taking lessons," she replied. "Miss Donovan is my teacher. I am in second beginners now." Jannie looked proud of herself.

"Me, too," I said. "I am in second beginners. But you were not in first beginners with me. You were not in my class."

"I know. The classes change," Jannie told me.

Boy, was she right. Here is who was in my new class: Sophie, Gregg, Polly, Gemma (four kids I did not know), Jannie, me, and Natalie Springer. Natalie is also in my class at school. She is nice. We are friends. But Natalie is a klutz. I could not imagine her doing gymnastics.

We sat down. Miss Donovan welcomed us to our new class. She explained what we were going to learn. I tried to pay attention. But mostly I looked at the other kids. Then Miss Donovan said we would have a review.

She asked us to turn a forward roll. I did a great job. So did Jannie and Gemma. (Natalie had to try twice.)

Miss Donovan asked us to walk along the low balance beam. I did a great job. So did Gregg and Polly. (Natalie fell off.)

Miss Donovan asked us to leap over the horse. (It is not a real horse.) I did a great job. So did Sophie and Jannie. (Natalie got stuck on top of the horse. She looked mad.)

Then Miss Donovan asked us to try a cartwheel. I still could not do one. My hands and feet got mixed up. Everyone else could turn a cartwheel. Even Natalie. (Well, sort of.) I would just have to keep practicing.

The Beautiful Family Contest

"Who can play with me? Who can play with me?" I called.

"I *can* play with you, Karen," said Sam, "but I do not *want* to."

"All right, who *wants* to play with me?" I called.

"I'm busy," Charlie replied.

"I have homework," Kristy replied.

"I am finishing my model airplane," said David Michael.

"I am trying to read," said Andrew. (That

might have been true. Andrew is trying to *learn* to read.)

Emily Michelle was not busy, but I did not feel like playing with her.

I sighed. Andrew and I were at Daddy's house for the weekend. I did not know what to do with myself. So I wandered into the playroom upstairs. I flopped onto the couch. I picked up a magazine. It was a grown-up magazine, but I looked at it anyway. The magazine was called *Beautiful Home*. On the cover was a picture of a very lovely dining room. With very lovely food on the table.

I opened the magazine and turned the pages. I saw lots of pictures of rooms and houses. The pictures were pretty, but they were boring. I was about to close the magazine when I saw the word CONTEST. I just love contests. I love them as much as holidays. So I stopped and read the page. This is what it said: *Do you have a beautiful family? Beautiful Home is searching for the beautiful family of the year. Win prizes! Get your picture in our magazine! To enter, follow these simple directions.*

Guess what first prize was — a trip to Hawaii. I have always wanted to go to Hawaii. I want to see a volcano. Also, I want to wear a lei. (That is a necklace made of flowers.) I want to put on a grass skirt and learn the hula dance.

Second prize was a vacuum cleaner, and third prize was a hat or something. I did not care about the vacuum or the hat. But I wanted to go to Hawaii. So I read the instructions for entering the contest. I would have to write a short essay about my beautiful family, and I would have to find a picture of us, too. Those things were easy, I thought. But which of my families would I enter in the contest? I decided on my big-house family. I think it is a teeny bit more interesting than my little-house family.

I found a pad of paper and began my essay. "I have one brother, three stepbroth-

ers, one stepsister, and an adopted sister,"
I wrote. "My family is very beautiful even
if my brothers are rude. They embarrass
me. Sam burps at the table. Andrew usually
spills stuff in restaurants. But I love my
brothers. I think we are a beautiful family
anyway. . . . "

"Karen?" called Daddy. "Bedtime!"

"Okay!" I called back. "Coming!"

I gathered up the magazine and my paper. I had decided not to tell anyone about
the contest. My brothers would tease me.
They would laugh at me. They would say
I would never get to go to Hawaii and dance
the hula.

I heard someone in the hallway.

Yikes! What should I do with my contest
things? I stuffed them underneath a cush-
ion in the couch. I could get them the next
day.

I walked slowly out of the playroom. My
heart was pounding. I had almost been
caught! But when I ran into Sam, I just said,

"Hi, Sam. Good night, Sam. See you in the morning."

And then I went to bed.

That night I dreamed of leis and grass skirts and volcanoes.

April Fools' Day

I like school. That is because of Ms. Colman. She is a gigundoly wonderful teacher. Ms. Colman hardly ever yells. She never makes kids feel embarrassed. She listens to us, she lets school be fun for her students, *and* she makes Surprising Announcements. (These are always good.) Sometimes Ms. Colman has to remind me to use my indoor voice when I am in school, but that is okay. I need to be reminded. I can get a little bit noisy. Lots of grown-ups tell me to use my indoor voice.

Another thing I like about my teacher is that she wears glasses. So do I. I even have two pairs. (I am a glasses two-two.) I always have to wear one pair. The blue pair is for reading or doing close-up work. The pink pair is for the rest of the time.

I did not used to need glasses. I just got them this year, in second grade. Before I got glasses, Ms. Colman let me sit in the back of our classroom. I sat with Hannie and Nancy. But after I started wearing glasses, Ms. Colman moved me to the front row. She wanted me to be able to see the blackboard better. (Our blackboard is green. I do not know *why* we don't call it the greenboard.) All the glasses-wearers sit in the front row. The other glasses-wearers are Natalie Springer (the one in my gymnastics class) and Ricky Torres. Ricky and I used to be enemies. Now we are . . . married! We decided we liked each other, so one day we held a wedding on the playground. (We are just pretend married, of course.)

Ricky's best friend is also in our class. His name is Bobby Gianelli. Sometimes Bobby is fun, and sometimes he is a big fat pain.

Like today in school. As soon as I came into the classroom, Bobby said, "Guess what, Karen. April Fools' Day is coming."

"Duh," I replied.

"I am going to get you."

"Well, I am going to get you back."

"I have big plans for you."

"*I* have big plans for *you*." I thought for a moment. Then I added, "Hey, Bobby, wait a second. You cannot get me, and I cannot get you. April Fools' Day is a Saturday. I know because I will be at my father's house then."

"Uh-oh," said Bobby.

This was very bad news.

"Hey, Hannie," I said, as soon as she sat at her desk. "Bad news. We will not be able to play April Fool jokes in school. April Fools' Day is a Saturday."

"Yikes," said Hannie. "And I thought of some good tricks."

"Me, too," spoke up Pamela Harding. (Pamela and I do not get along very well. Except for sometimes.) "I know a great joke to play."

"So do I," said Hank Reubens and Leslie Morris and the twins, Tammy and Terri.

"I have an idea," said Nancy. "Maybe Ms. Colman will let us celebrate April Fools' Day on Friday. You know, on April Fools' Day Eve."

"Yeah!" I exclaimed. "We could do that. It would not matter."

As soon as Ms. Colman came into our room, we asked her about April Fools' Day. She said we could play our tricks on Friday. She reminded us about not playing mean jokes and not hurting anybody.

Whew. That was a relief. I could play tricks in school *and* at the big house. I paused. Hmm. *Should* I play tricks on my big-house family? After all, I had entered us in the Beautiful Family contest. I had finished my essay. I had found two good photographs. And I had mailed everything to the contest people. If my family was going to help me win a trip to Hawaii, maybe I should be extra nice to them.

The Mail Truck

"Thank you, Mrs. Dawes! 'Bye, Nancy! See you later!"

School was over. Mrs. Dawes had driven Nancy and me home. I ran next door to the little house. When I reached our front stoop, Andrew bounded outside.

"Karen! The mail has not come yet!" he cried.

"Oh, goody!" I replied.

Andrew and I like to get mail. Even better, we like to meet the mail truck. But the mail truck usually comes while I am at school and Andrew is at preschool. Today, we could wait for it.

I never know what might arrive in the mail. Maybe a letter from Maxie, my pen pal. Or a letter from my grandparents in the state of Nebraska. Or a really interesting magazine. Or even a package!

Andrew and I got a snack in the kitchen. Then we sat on the front stoop and ate our apples and raisins. Pretty soon Andrew jumped up. He said, "Here comes the mail truck!" Then he added, "Hold onto your hats!"

My brother and I raced across our yard.

Squeak, squeak went the brakes of the mail truck.

"Hello, hello!" we called.

"Hello!" replied Mrs. Ramirez. She is our letter carrier. She handed me a stack of letters. Then she handed Andrew a box.

"Quick, Karen!" exclaimed Andrew. "Read the box. Who is it for?"

"Hey, it's for us!" I said. "It is from McBuzz's Mail Order."

We said good-bye to Mrs. Ramirez. We ran inside. I gave the letters to Mommy. Then Andrew and I tore open the box from McBuzz's.

"Here is my camera!" shrieked Andrew. He opened a plug in the bottom of the plastic camera. He filled the camera with water. "Say cheese!" he said to me.

"Cheese!" I pretended to pose for a picture.

Squeep! A stream of water squirted me in the face.

We looked in the box again. I pulled out the plastic cockroach. "Do you know what I am going to do with this?" I asked Andrew. "I am going to take it to school on April Fools' Day Eve. I am going to get Bobby Gianelli with it. I will wait until gym is over. I will hide the bug in his shoe. Then when he takes off his sneakers and changes into his shoes, his foot will squish right on the bug!"

"Ew," said Andrew. He looked in the box again. He took out the trick soap and the trick gum and the trick ice cube and the rubber spider.

April Fools' Day was going to be gigundoly fun.

I was really going to get Bobby Gianelli.

No Fun

I watched the kids in my gymnastics class. Our class had not started yet. We were waiting for Gemma and Jannie to arrive. While we waited, we practiced turning cartwheels. Polly was the best. Gregg was the next best. He and Polly just went right over, with their legs high in the air. I tried two cartwheels. Both times, I bent my knees. My legs fell down. I looked like a crab.

When Gemma and Jannie showed up, Miss Donovan began our class. She asked

us to sit on one of the tumbling mats. I sat between Polly and Sophie.

"Today," said Miss Donovan, "we are going to work on floor exercises. Each of you is going to learn a short routine."

That sounded like fun. I turned to Polly. I wanted to say, "Oh, cool," to her. That is what I would have said to Dana. But Dana was not in my class anymore. And Polly was not looking at me. She was watching Miss Donovan.

I looked in the other direction, at Sophie. She was watching Miss Donovan, too. I sighed. I felt as if I were not a part of my new class. I wanted to be friends with all the other kids.

I nudged Sophie. "Do you like April Fools' Day?" I whispered.

Sophie glanced at me. "I guess so," she whispered back.

"I am going to play some good jokes."

"Mm-hmm."

"I bought trick soap and trick gum and a rubber bug."

"Yup."

"I got them from this catalog. It's called McBuzz's Mail Order."

Sophie glanced at me again. "Shhh! I cannot hear Miss Donovan," she said.

Well. What nerve. I decided to leave Sophie alone. Maybe Polly would be my gymnastics friend. "Hey, Polly," I whispered.

"Yeah?" Polly did not look at me. Miss Donovan was showing us how to do a handstand. Polly was watching closely.

"At my school we are going to play April Fools' tricks on Friday," I told Polly. "April Fools' Day is really on Saturday, but we want to celebrate in school, too. I thought of a way cool trick to play on — "

Polly raised her hand. "Miss Donovan?" she said. "Can you please show us the handstand again? I need to see something."

Well. What nerve. I decided to leave Polly alone, too. Maybe Gregg would be my gymnastics friend. Gregg was sitting in front of me. I poked him.

Gregg turned around. "What?"

"Do you get McBuzz's Mail Order?" I asked him.

Now Gregg raised his hand. "Miss Donovan?" he said. "Karen Brewer is bothering me. She will not let me pay attention."

"Karen, please keep quiet," said Miss Donovan.

Humph. I decided I did not like my new gymnastics class at all. The kids were mean. They did not want to be my friends.

I glanced around at them. Not one was looking at me. They were all watching Miss Donovan. Well, if they were going to ignore me, then I would ignore them back. I would even ignore Natalie and Jannie. But only in gymnastics school. Not in regular school.

After awhile Miss Donovan let us stand up. We did some stretching exercises. Then we practiced the floor routine.

"Karen," said Natalie. "Can you do a split?"

"Karen," said Gemma. "Could you help me?"

"Karen," said Sophie. "I did not hear Miss Donovan's instructions. What did she say?"

I did not answer any of them. I did not even talk to Miss Donovan.

"Look at Me!"

Roll, roll, roll, "Ta-dah!"

I turned three forward rolls in a row, then jumped to my feet and took a bow. I had started rolling in the hallway of the big house, and I landed in the den. Kristy was there playing Candy Land with Andrew and Emily Michelle. "You landed on red," she said to Emily.

"Ta-dah!" I cried again.

"Oh," said Kristy. "Very nice, Karen." She went back to the game.

Boo.

I left the den. I ran into the living room. Sam and Charlie were there. "Look at me!" I exclaimed. I put one leg forward and one leg back, and I slid into a split. Sort of. Halfway down my knees bent.

"Gee, that's great, Karen," said Charlie.

"Yeah. You ought to be in the Olympics," added Sam.

"Meanie-moes," I said.

I ran upstairs to the playroom. David Michael was there with Shannon. He was teaching Shannon to sit up and give her paw.

"Look at me!" I cried. I turned a backward roll. It was perfect.

"What a cinch," muttered David Michael. "Anybody can do that."

This was not true. I could do it because of gymnastics. I could do it because I had taken first beginners, and now I was in second beginners.

So far, I had gone to pretty many of my new gymnastics classes. I still did not talk to the kids. But I was learning a lot. My

forward rolls and backward rolls were great. I could do lots of things on the balance beam. I could do some things on the little trampoline. (But I could not turn a cartwheel.)

Maybe I should practice.

I ran back downstairs. I cartwheeled into the den. (I landed on my bottom.)

"Ha, ha," said Andrew.

I cartwheeled into the living room. (I landed on my bottom again.)

"Good job," said Sam.

I cartwheeled into the kitchen. Daddy and Elizabeth and Nannie were there. They were drinking coffee.

I landed on my feet. Even so, Daddy said, "Honey, not in the kitchen, please."

And Nannie added, "I nearly spilled my coffee. You surprised me."

"Sorry," I said.

I went to my bedroom.

I decided my family was rude. Especially my brothers.

Sam had made fun of me. Charlie had

teased me. David Michael had been mean to me. Andrew had laughed at me. And that was not all. Daddy and Elizabeth and Nannie did not care about my cartwheels. Kristy did not care about my three forward rolls in a row. I could not tell whether Emily cared. She had not said anything. I decided she probably did not care. She could have said, "Yea!" or clapped her hands. But she had played Candy Land instead.

"Everybody is mean," I said to Moosie. "Plus, everyone forgets their manners. Do you know what David Michael did at dinner tonight? He stabbed his baked potato with his fork, and then he waved the potato around and called it a Popsicle. So then Andrew copied him. Only his potato fell off the fork and hit Sam's arm and Sam poked Andrew and Andrew cried and Emily got mad and threw her plate on the floor. Isn't that disgusting? My family will never win the Beautiful Family contest. They are *too* rude. Because of them I will not get to dance the hula in Hawaii."

Karen's Big Joke

"That is not fair," I told Moosie. "I want to go to Hawaii. I *could* go to Hawaii, if my family had manners. If they were a Beautiful Family. Hmm. I wonder if I could *make* them beautiful, Moosie."

Moosie said he was not sure. He said I should try, though.

At breakfast on Saturday, I said, "David Michael, please chew with your mouth closed. You are giving me Lookies."

"I like to give you Lookies," my brother replied. He shoveled some scrambled eggs

42

into his mouth. Then he added some blue-
berries. He chewed everything up. He
opened his mouth. "Lookie!" he said.

"Oh, gross!" I cried. "Daddy, David Michael gave me an egg-and-blueberry
Lookie. It was yellow and blue. It was turning green."

"Daddy, Karen is a tattletale," said
Andrew.

"Oh, everybody be quiet," I said.

Breakfast was almost over when Sam sat
back in his chair. He opened his mouth. He
made a gigundo burp.

"Sam!" I exclaimed.

My family was not getting any more
beautiful.

Later that morning, Charlie said, "Who
wants to help me wash the Junk Bucket?"
The Junk Bucket is Charlie's beat-up old
car. It really does look like a bucket of junk.

"Me!" said Emily.

"I do!" said Andrew.

"I do, too!" said David Michael.

I did not want to help. But I wanted to

watch. I sat on the front steps of the big house. Emily and my brothers put on their oldest clothes. They found buckets and sponges. Charlie dragged out the hose.

"Okay, let's wash 'er up!" said Charlie. (He meant the Junk Bucket.)

Andrew grabbed the hose. He tripped over a bucket of water.

Emily squeezed soap onto her head. "Shampoo!" she cried.

The Junk Bucket looked as Junky as ever. No one was washing it.

I sighed. My family was a mess, and so was the car.

Even our pets were not beautiful. When I went into the house, I met Boo-Boo. He had just come through the cat door.

He was carrying a mole in his mouth. The mole was dead.

"Ew, ew, ew! Disgusting!" I shrieked.

"Karen? What is wrong?" asked Elizabeth.

"This family is disgusting," I replied. "Boo-Boo caught a mole. He brought it in-

44

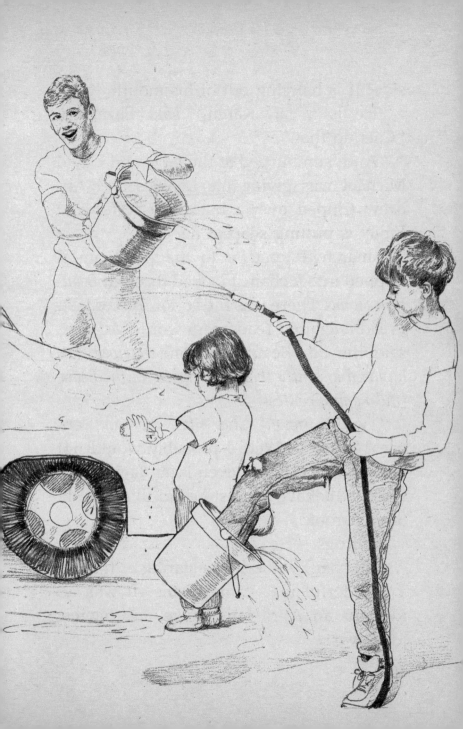

side. It is hanging out of his mouth."

"He is a cat, Karen," said Elizabeth. "Cats do that."

"And Sam burped at the table and David Michael was giving me Lookies and Andrew tripped over a bucket of water and Emily is putting soap in her hair."

I marched upstairs to the playroom. I flopped into a chair. I looked through *Beautiful Home*. There was the ad for the contest. I read it again. I read every word. *Last year*, said the ad, Beautiful Home *received two hundred and fifty thousand entries in the Beautiful Family contest*.

"Two hundred and fifty *thousand* entries?" I cried. Well. I probably would not win a trip to Hawaii even if my family was the best behaved, most beautiful family in Stoneybrook.

Bullfrogs.

And then, while I was staring at the ad, a wonderful idea came to me. It was an idea for an April Fools' joke, my biggest joke ever.

Head Up, Back Straight

I walked back and forth across the low balance beam. Each time I came to the end of the beam, I turned around carefully. In the old days, when I was a first beginner, I hopped off the beam at each end. I turned around on the mat. Then I climbed on the beam again. Now I could turn around *on* the *beam*. I did it very gracefully. I held out my arms. I kept my back straight. I kept my head up. If I remembered, I pointed my toes.

"Hey, Karen, that was good," said Gemma.

"Thanks," I mumbled.

"Will you show me how to turn around like that?" she asked.

I said, "I guess," but just as I did, Miss Donovan said something, too. She said, "Boys and girls, let's start class now."

That was all right with me. Ever since I had stopped talking to the kids in my class, I had been learning an awful lot of things. Like how to turn around at the end of the beam. I was ready to get to work.

But Miss Donovan had different plans than usual that day. First, she divided us into three groups: Polly, Gemma, and I were Group I. Jannie, Gregg, and Sophie were Group II. Natalie and Miss Donovan were Group III. (I think maybe Miss Donovan wanted to give Natalie some extra help.)

Next, Miss Donovan said, "Who knows what a spotter is?"

Natalie waved her hand around wildly.

"It's like a bug," she said, "and it has eight legs and there are lots of kinds — "

Gregg interrupted her. "Not *spider*," he said. "Spotter. *Spot-ter*. Miss Donovan asked what a spotter is."

Natalie blushed. "Sor-reee," she said.

"That's okay." Miss Donovan smiled. "A spotter," she went on, "is a person who watches while another person is practicing a move on a piece of equipment or trying a floor exercise. A spotter helps the gymnast. Most important, he keeps his eye on the gymnast at *all* times. He is right there if the gymnast stumbles or falls or runs into any trouble. A good spotter is very important. Each of you should learn to be a good spotter."

Miss Donovan showed us some things about spotting. Then she let the groups work on their own. Group II worked on the trampoline. My group worked on the beam. Miss Donovan helped Natalie with the floor routine.

Boo. If I was going to be a good spotter, I would probably have to talk to Polly and Gemma. All right, I will only talk when I have to, I thought.

Gemma ran to the balance beam. She hopped onto one end. "This is great, Karen," she said. "Now you can show me how to turn around."

"Mm-hmm," I replied.

I walked with Gemma to the end of the beam. I did not help her by taking her hand, but I walked next to her, the way Miss Donovan had shown us. I held out my hand, just in case.

At the end of the beam, Gemma turned around carefully.

"Good," I said. "That's right. See? Keep your head up and your back straight. Try it again at the other end."

I helped Polly with the turn, too.

Later, when we practiced our floor routines, I spotted Polly and showed her a good way to turn forward rolls. Then she spotted me and helped me with my cart-wheels. Polly and Gemma and I worked hard.

Also, we talked a lot, but I did not realize that until class was over. I realized something else then, too. The kids in Miss Donovan's class like to talk — about gymnastics. After all, that is why they were in class.

"Made You Look!"

"**H**ey, Andrew!" I called. "Quick! Look outside! A gorilla is in the front yard! It is dancing around. . . . Now it is waving to me!"

Andrew ran to his bedroom window. "Where? Where is the gorilla?" he cried.

"April Fool!" I said.

Friday had arrived at last. But —

"Today is not April Fools' Day," said my brother. "No fair."

"It is April Fools' Day in Ms. Colman's room," I told him.

"Well, we are at Mommy's house. We are not at your school."

Boo. Andrew was no fun.

School was fun, though. Andrew let me borrow his squirting camera. I put it in my schoolbag along with the trick soap, the trick gum, and of course, the plastic cockroach. Today was my day to get Bobby Gianelli.

This is what I did the very second I stepped inside Ms. Colman's room. I called to Hannie. "Hey, Hannie, your shoe is untied!"

"Uh-oh," Hannie answered. She leaned over to fix her laces.

"April Fool! Made you look!" I shouted.

Hannie was wearing loafers. (They did not have shoelaces.) She giggled. "You got me, Karen."

April Fools' Day Eve was off to a great start.

I sat at my desk. I put away the things in my book bag. I had not told *any*one about what I had ordered from McBuzz's. I waited for a moment. Then I took out Andrew's camera. It was already filled with water. When Pamela Harding walked into the room, I smiled.

"Ooh, Pamela, what a lovely dress," I said. "May I take your picture?"

"Sure!" Pamela looked pleased.

I pressed the button on top of the camera.

Squeep! The little stream of water shot into Pamela's hair.

"Ew! Oh, gross! Karen, you ruined my hair!" cried Pamela. (There was, like, one drop of water on Pamela's hair.)

All around us, kids were laughing. "April Fool!" I said.

Pamela frowned. She flumped into her chair.

"Is that how you are going to get *me?*" Bobby asked me. "Because now I have already seen your tricks."

"Maybe, maybe not. Maybe, maybe not," I sang.

Soon school began. Ms. Colman made a Surprising Awful Announcement. "This weekend," she said, "I want you to do five math worksheets and write a report about transportation."

Transportation? *Five* worksheets? Oh, yuck!

"April Fool!" cried Ms. Colman. She had gotten us.

All morning I waited for gym. I tried to be patient. That was hard, considering I had hidden the cockroach in my shoe. I could feel it every time I moved my foot. At last Ms. Colman told our class to line up for P. E. (That stands for physical education.) We walked to the gym. We took off our shoes. We put on our sneakers. I tied my laces very, very slowly. While I did that, Bobby ran for a basketball. He and Ricky and Hank tossed it around.

I dropped the bug in Bobby's shoe. I pushed it down into the toe.

In gym class, we played with a parachute. Then we practiced climbing ropes. When class ended, we ran to change out of our sneakers.

Bobby stuck his sock foot into one of his shoes. He frowned. Then he reached into the shoe and pulled out the cockroach. "Aughhh!" he screamed.

"April Fool, Bobby!" I cried. "I got you!"

Beware, Karen!

"Okay, now I am *really* going to get you," said Bobby.

We were leaving the gym. I was holding the cockroach. Bobby's face was red. But he was laughing. He could not believe he had been fooled by a silly plastic bug. I dangled it in front of him. The roach did not even look real. Its head was covered with fur.

"Just wait until lunchtime," whispered Bobby.

Hmm. What a good clue!

At lunchtime I was on my guard. I sat with Nancy, Hannie, Natalie, and the twins in the cafeteria. I bought the school lunch. It was spaghetti and salad and milk. The dessert was rice pudding. Before I began to eat, I checked my food carefully. I wanted to be sure Bobby had not hidden anything in it. Or done anything to it.

My lunch looked fine.

That was why I did not panic later when Bobby leaned over from the next table and stared at my dessert. "Ew!" he cried. "A fly landed in your pudding!"

I barely looked at the pudding. "Bobby," I said. (I sighed loudly.) "That is a raisin. There are raisins in your pudding, too."

"Darn it," replied Bobby.

I picked the raisin out of my pudding. I put it on Hannie's napkin. "Ew!" I exclaimed. "Ew, Hannie, a huge pudding-covered fly landed on your tray. It is heading for your spaghetti!"

Then I picked another raisin out of my pudding. I put it on Nancy's napkin. "Nancy! Fly alert!" I cried.

My friends and I were giggling. We could not stop.

Bobby turned back to his own lunch. Every so often, though, he would look over his shoulder at me. He waited until I had finished eating. Then he said, "Hey, Karen, want some ABC gum?"

"Why, Bobby, how nice of you to offer," I replied. "No, thank you."

Bobby could not fool me. I know what ABC gum is. ABC stands for Already Been Chewed. Bobby was going to pull his own gum out of his mouth and give me half of it. Yuck.

Bobby and his friends left the cafeteria. They went to the playground for recess. A little while later, the Three Musketeers went outside, too. The first thing we saw was a bunch of boys crowded around something on the ground. Bobby was with them.

"Karen!" he yelled. "Come here!"

"Watch out for another trick," Nancy whispered to me.

"Karen, we found buried treasure!" Bobby shouted. "Right here on the playground. I think it is a pirate's chest."

"Yeah, right," I said.

"No, really. Come here. . . . I will give you a piece of gold."

"Are you April Fooling, Bobby?" I said.

After recess, my friends and I returned to our class. Bobby ran ahead of us. When I reached my desk, he was standing behind my chair. "Allow me to seat you," he said politely.

"Goodness, Bobby. Thanks," I answered. But I did not sit down.

"What are you waiting for?" Bobby asked.

"My chair. I know you pulled it away." I looked behind me. Sure enough, Bobby had moved my chair. If I had sat down, I would have landed on the floor.

"April Fool!" I said to Bobby. "You can't get me!"

When school was over, Bobby *still* had not tricked me.

I was the April Fools' Day queen.

The Gymnastics Team

"Karen?"

"Yeah?"

"I asked you a question," said Miss Donovan.

Oops. I was in my gymnastics class. I was not paying attention. I was thinking about my big joke. "Sorry," I said to my teacher. "What did you say?"

"I asked everyone if they have been practicing at home."

"Oh, yes," I said. "All the time. In the basement of my mother's house."

Miss Donovan smiled. She began talking again.

But I stopped listening.

I remembered the joke I had played on Andrew that morning. I remembered fooling Bobby in gym class. I thought about the tricks Bobby had *tried* to play on me. Then I thought about my big joke.

It was all planned. I was going to play it the next day, on the real April Fools' Day. But I was going to start it that night at dinner with my big-house family.

This was my joke. I had already decided that I probably would not win first prize in the contest and get to go to Hawaii. I probably would not win no matter how beautiful my family was. But my family would not know that. They did not know how many people had entered the contest. They did not even know that I had entered the contest. So I would tell them. And then I would say that a judge had called me and maybe I was a winner, but I would not find out for sure until the judge had come to the big house to see my beautiful family himself.

I bet everyone in my family would get very dressed up. They would clean their rooms. They would be on their best behavior, waiting for the judge. But the judge would never arrive! April Fools' Day was going to be gigundoly fun.

In gymnastics class, Sophie and I practiced on the trampoline. We practiced very hard. Sometimes I wanted to stop and say to Sophie, "Guess what April Fool tricks I played today." But I did not. Instead, I kept working. I said to Sophie, "Tuck your chin down when you turn over on the rings." I spotted her carefully.

Sophie grinned at me. "We are pretty good gymnasts, aren't we, Karen?"

"Yeah. I think so. If I could just turn a cartwheel."

"But you can do a back flip on the mat," Sophie reminded me. "No one else in our class can do that."

That was true.

Before class ended, Miss Donovan said

she wanted us to have a meeting. We had never held a meeting at gymnastics.

"Please sit on the tumbling mats," said our teacher.

We sat down. Gemma asked me to sit next to her, and so did Polly. I sat between them. We waited for Miss Donovan to start talking.

"Class," she said, "I am happy to be able to tell you about a special gymnastics team our school is forming. It is called an invitational team. That means you must be *invited* to join it."

"And *that* means you have to be really good," I whispered to Gemma and Polly.

"The team will participate in gymnastics meets all over Connecticut," Miss Donovan went on. "One or two students from every class in school will be asked to join the team. During the next few weeks I will be watching each of you closely. Some of the other teachers may come to our class and watch you, too. Try not to feel nervous. Just do your best."

I wondered if my best was good enough. I *really* wanted to be on the special team and travel around Connecticut with my new friends. I was excited — but when class ended, I began thinking about my big joke again.

Finalists

"Everybody, I have an annoucement," I said.

Gymnastics was over. Mommy had driven Andrew and me to Daddy's for the weekend. My big-house family and I were eating supper in the kitchen. We were eating chicken and vegetables.

I had decided that Ms. Colman should not be the only one who gets to make Surprising Announcements. I would make one, too.

"You got your own apartment?" Sam asked me.

"No, silly," I replied. I cleared my throat. I wanted to say this just right. "A few weeks ago," I began, "I entered a contest. I saw it in *Beautiful Home* magazine. It was called the Beautiful Family contest. I wrote an essay about why my family was beautiful and special. My big-house family, I mean. And I sent in a photo of us. First prize in the contest is a trip to Hawaii. There are a bunch of other prizes, too."

Sam snorted. "Like you are really going to go to Hawaii, Karen."

I smiled. "I might," I said. "That is my announcement. I got a letter from the contest people yesterday. Guess what. We may be winners. Anyway, we are finalists. A judge might come over tomorrow to meet us and to look at our house and yard. So we better be neat and clean. And well-behaved," I added. "We will have to impress that judge."

"Karen," said Daddy. "Are you sure about this?"

"Of course I am."

"Could I see the letter?"

"Um, I left it in my desk. I took it to school to show my friends."

"How come you did not tell us about the contest until now?" asked Charlie.

"I wanted to surprise you," I told him.

"Honey, I don't know," said Elizabeth. "I do not like the idea of a stranger showing up at our house to look around."

"Um, I think he will call first," I said. "He will tell you about the contest. He will probably call tomorrow morning."

"All right," said Daddy. "Please let me speak to the judge when he phones."

"Okay!" I said.

I ran to my room. This was the beginning of my big joke. It was going to be a really good one, I could tell. And it was only April Fools' Day Eve.

"Get ready for tomorrow," I whispered to Moosie.

The Big Fuss

"Eek, a snake! Oh, my heavens! A snake is in the bathroom!"

Elizabeth was shouting. That is what woke me up on Saturday morning. At first I just lay under my covers. Then I leaped out of bed. I flew down the hallway. If a snake was in our bathroom, I wanted to see it.

"Where? Where, Elizabeth?" I cried.

David Michael and Kristy were right behind me. "Where, Mom?" they said.

Elizabeth grinned at us. "April Fool!"

"Good one, Mom," said Kristy.

I was laughing. "Yeah, good one. First thing in the morning, too."

At breakfast, David Michael put salt in the sugar bowl. "April Fool!" he cried when Nannie spit out her coffee.

Then Andrew got Kristy with the squirting camera. "April Fool!" he cried.

Then Kristy said she would fix cereal for me. She served me a bowl of chicken noodle soup. "April Fool!" she cried.

After that, Emily began saying. "April Fool!" Only she said, "Apra Foo!" And I do not think she understood about tricks and jokes.

First she pinched Sam and cried, "Apra Foo!"

Then she scared Andrew and cried, "Apra Foo!"

When I got tired of Emily's Apra Foos, I ran upstairs. I telephoned Hannie. "Hi, it's me," I whispered.

"Hi," Hannie answered. "Why are you whispering?"

"I will tell you later. Can you call me right back?"

"Sure. Why?"

"I will tell you later."

"Okay."

Hannie called back. I picked up the phone. I pretended to sound very excited. "Oh, really? Oh, *really?*" I exclaimed. "Oh, my goodness. I do not believe it! Thank you very much. Good-bye!" Then I whispered to Hannie, "I'm coming over later. I will explain everything."

I hung up the phone and ran back downstairs. "Guess what, everybody!" I cried. "That was the judge! He just called. And he will be by sometime today to inspect us. We — "

"Karen," Daddy interrupted. "I wanted to talk to the judge."

"Oh. I'm sorry. I forget about that. But isn't this exciting news?"

"*I* think it is!" said Nannie. "We better get to work. We should weed the flower gardens. We should tidy up the playroom.

We should change our clothes."

"I will fix my tux," said Sam.

"So will I," said Charlie.

"Maybe I will go to the beauty parlor," said Elizabeth.

"Can I wear jeans?" asked Kristy.

"Not if you want to win the contest," Sam told her. "Not if you want to go to Hawaii. Or get . . . What is second prize, Karen?"

"Oh, it does not matter," I said.

"Of course not," replied Sam. "Because we are going to go to Hawaii."

"Yea!" cheered David Michael.

So everyone became very busy.

I ran to my room and changed into my best dress.

The Giggles

While I was changing, I wanted to laugh. My brothers were looking for their tuxes. Daddy and Nannie were probably already weeding the gardens. David Michael and Andrew and Emily were putting their toys away.

So far, everyone believed my big joke.

But I did not laugh. I did not want to ruin anything. I went downstairs and found Elizabeth. (She was cleaning the oven.)

"I am going over to Hannie's," I announced. "I want to tell her about the judge

75

and the contest. I am all ready for the judge," I added. "See?" I twirled around. "I will come back before the judge gets here."

"Okay," said Elizabeth. "Stay clean. You might not have time to change again. Be careful of your good clothes."

Hannie and I lay on her bedroom floor. (I had forgotten about my good clothes.) We lay on our stomachs, facing each other.

"Why are you so dressed up?" Hannie wanted to know.

I grinned. Then I told her about the big joke.

Hannie began to laugh. "So your family is getting ready for the judge's visit? What are you going to do now?"

"As soon as I get home, I will shout 'April Fool!' "

Hannie was still laughing. "And everyone will be dressed up, and your house will look gorgeous," she said.

"Yes. At last my family will have some manners."

"Sam will not burp," said Hannie.

"Charlie will not tease," I said. "And no one will look sloppy."

"Wouldn't it have been cool if you had *really* won the contest, though?" asked Hannie.

"Way cool," I answered. "I would have let you come to Hawaii with us. We could have taken hula lessons together."

"Oh, well. I guess it does not matter too much. You know why?"

"Why?" I asked.

"Because we got a pony."

"A pony!" I exclaimed.

Hannie nodded. "I didn't tell you before, because I was saving it for a surprise. Want to see the pony? He's in the backyard."

I leaped up. I scrambled across the room to Hannie's window. "Where is he?" I asked. I wanted to ride him.

Hannie joined me at the window. "He's right over there."

"Where?"

"There."

"There? I do not see anything."

"April Fool!" shrieked Hannie.

"Hannie!" I exclaimed, laughing. "You really got me!"

I was dirty and rumpled from lying on the floor. Oh, well. That did not matter much. My joke was almost over. We sat on Hannie's bed. "Of course, you know why I believed you, don't you?" I said.

"No. Why?"

"Because of Seth's parrot. He is getting a *talking* parrot today. I thought if Seth was getting a parrot, you could have gotten a horse."

"Seth is getting a *par*rot?" exclaimed Hannie.

"Nope. April Fool!"

Hannie and I were laughing so hard, tears were running down our cheeks. We rolled around on her bed. We rolled around until Hannie rolled onto the floor with a THUD and her father called, "Girls, what is going on up there?" Then we calmed down.

I looked at my watch. Yipes. I had been at Hannie's house a *long* time. "Hannie, I better go home," I said quickly. "I think my joke is over. I am ready to fool my big-house family. I will ring our doorbell. They will think the judge has come. When they open the door, I will yell, 'April Fool!' "

The Disaster

I was standing at our front door.

My heart was going *thumpety-thumpety-thumpety-thumpety*. It felt as if it might jump right out of my chest.

I rang the bell.

While I waited for someone to open the door, I noticed something about our yard. It did not look all that neat. I did not think Daddy or Nannie had weeded anything. Also, some papers had blown onto the grass. They were just lying there. Our doormat was dirty. And a bunch of Emily's toys

81

were cluttering up the driveway. Plus the Junk Bucket was parked where anyone could see it.

Oh, well. My big-house family must have spent the morning getting fixed up. And also fixing up the inside of the house. It probably looked gorgeous. I smiled at the thought.

I heard footsteps at the door. It was flung open by Sam. I could not believe what I saw.

"Sam!" I gasped. "What are you — "

Sam interrupted me. "Oh, it's you, Karen. How come you are ringing the bell? You do not have to ring the bell at your own house."

"Sam, my gosh — "

"Oh, it does not matter. Come on inside. The judge from the contest is here. He got here a few minutes ago."

What judge from the contest? How could that be? I made that up, didn't I? Yikes, what if we really *were* finalists in the contest? What if the contest people had loved my entry, and I had been chosen from those thousands and thousands of people?

Oh, my goodness! I was going to Hawaii after all! I could learn to hula, and I could wear a lei and see a volcano. I could bring Hannie and Nancy with me.

But something was wrong. Sam. Sam was wrong. That was what I had started to say when he opened the door for me. Sam was not wearing his tuxedo. He was not dressed up at all. He was wearing the same grubby outfit he had been wearing at breakfast. Jeans with a hole at each knee, and a shirt that he'd ripped the sleeves from so it would be cooler, and sneakers that *fwap-fwapped* when he walked, because the rubber soles were coming apart from the tops of the shoes. His hair looked as if it had been combed with an electric toothbrush. And his hands were dirty.

I grabbed Sam by the tail of his torn shirt. "Where is your tux?" I whispered. I slammed the door closed behind me.

"I didn't have time to find it," Sam re-

plied. (He did not sound sorry about that.) "Nannie did not have a chance to weed, either."

"I could tell."

"And my mom did not make it to the beauty parlor. And Emily is not quite dressed yet. And Andrew tried to give himself a haircut."

Uh-oh.

"Oh, well," said Sam. "I guess it could be worse."

I did not see how.

Sam led me into the living room. My big-house family was there. So was a tall man wearing a suit. Right away, I saw that he was the *only* one wearing a suit. Daddy was in his old Saturday outfit. Charlie's clothes looked as bad as Sam's. Andrew was still wearing his pajamas. Emily was wearing a saggy diaper and a T-shirt.

I did not look so hot myself.

Even so, I said to the man, "Hi. I am Karen Brewer. And this is my beautiful family."

The Biggest Mess

"Nice to meet you, Karen," the judge replied. "My name is Joseph Sand."

I put on my very best manners. Even if I did not look nice, I could act nice. "Allow me to introduce you," I said to Mr. Sand.

I dragged Nannie over to him. I chose Nannie first, because at least she was wearing a dress. "Mr. Sand, this is my step-grandmother. I call her Nannie. We all do."

Nannie stuck out her right hand. "Sorry it is wet," she said. "I was doing the dishes. The ones from last week. Oh, well. Better

late than never, I guess. Next week I will wash this week's dishes."

I wondered if I looked as horrified as Mr. Sand did.

Probably, I decided. But I introduced the rest of my family. Daddy's hands were covered with grease. He did not even wipe them on his pants before he shook hands with Mr. Sand. Andrew would not shake Mr. Sand's hand at all. Emily cried. Sam burped. He did not say, "Excuse me." He just laughed.

I had to do something fast.

"Mr. Sand, may I show you around our house and yard?" I asked.

I was not sure that was such a great idea. But it had to be better than standing around with my piggy family.

Guess what. My family followed us around. They came along on the tour of the house and yard. Even though it was really the judge's tour.

I led the judge upstairs. On the way, I

thought about which room to show off first. Not my own. I had not finished cleaning it up. I decided on Andrew's. He had cleaned *his* up. Plus, he is pretty neat anyway.

"Mr. Sand, this is my brother Andrew's beautiful room." I showed him inside. "Yipes!" I cried. "Oh, my goodness!"

Andrew's room was not neat. In fact, I could hardly walk through it. The floor was covered with Legos and Lincoln Logs and Tinker Toys. Since Andrew was right behind me, I cried, "What happened?"

"My building fell down," he answered.

"Let's look at another room, Mr. Sand," I suggested.

We peeked into Sam's. The room looked like a laundry had exploded in it. Clothes were everywhere. They were even draped over his lamps.

"No need to see that after all," I said quickly. "Let's try a bathroom."

Emily Michelle had been finger-painting in the bathroom. The tub and the tiles were red and blue and yellow.

Emily leaned into the bathroom. "I do that!" she exclaimed.

"You are supposed to clean up your messes!" I snapped.

Emily burst into tears. "Go away!" she cried.

Good idea.

"Mr. Sand, allow me to show you the yard," I said.

The judge and I stood on the back porch. We looked across the lawn. "My daddy planted those gardens," I said, pointing. "There is his flower garden, and there is his herb garden."

"What is that?" asked Mr. Sand. He was pointing at something else.

It was Boo-Boo. And he had caught a bird. He was trotting through the grass with the bird hanging out of his mouth. Oh, gross.

"Boo-Boo!" I shrieked.

Boo-Boo dropped the bird. He ran away.

I glanced at Mr. Sand. Mr. Sand was not

smiling. He was frowning. I thought about showing him our toolshed. I decided not to.

I knew I would never see the shores of Hawaii.

The Pig Family

I brought Mr. Sand back inside. We were standing in the kitchen.

"Would you like to stay for lunch?" Elizabeth asked the judge. She sounded very polite. But her hair was piled on her head in rollers. Also, she had said she was cold, but instead of a sweater, she had slipped her bathrobe over her jeans and shirt.

I was sure Mr. Sand would say no, he did not want to stay.

But before he could answer, Elizabeth

took him by the shoulders and sat him on one of the benches at our kitchen table. "Of course you must stay," she said. "Our house is yours. Make yourself at home."

"Elizabeth," I whispered, "shouldn't we eat in the dining room? The kitchen is sort of messy." (It was a wreck.)

"Honey, Mr. Sand does not mind."

"But *I* — " I started to say.

Too late. My family was sliding into their places at the table.

"What can I get you, Mr. Sand?" asked Daddy. "How about leftovers? That is what I am going to have. Nice leftover hash and nice leftover apple pie and nice leftover baloney."

"Daddy, I think the baloney is moldy," I said.

"Oh, well, Mr. Sand can just scrape off the green places, can't you?"

"I suppose so," answered the judge. He looked green himself.

"Hey, there's Boo-Boo!" said David Michael.

"Boo-Boo, perfect timing," said Nannie. "I think he wants his lunch. He missed out on his bird." Nannie opened one of those cans of smelly cat food. She dumped it into a dish. And Boo-Boo jumped onto the table. He landed practically on Mr. Sand's plate. "You really *are* hungry," Nannie said to Boo-Boo. And she let Boo-Boo eat *on the table*.

"I hungry!" announced Emily. She blew a raspberry.

"Me, too," said Sam. Then he bu-u-u-urped.

"You know what *I* want for lunch?" said Kristy. "I want . . . *great big globs of greasy grimy gopher's guts!*"

David Michael joined in. *"Little birdies' dirty feet! Mutilated monkey's meat. Great big globs of greasy grimy gopher's guts!"* he sang.

"And me without a spoon!" Charlie finished the song.

"Here you go, Mr. Sand." Daddy set a plate in front of the judge. On it were three pieces of moldy baloney and a knife. "You know what the knife is for, don't you?" He winked.

I turned to Kristy, who was sitting next to me. "Pinch me," I said.

"Why?"

"Because I must be dreaming. This is a nightmare."

When lunch was almost over, I said, "I guess we do not have any dessert for Mr. Sand, do we?"

"Why, Karen, of course we do," said Nannie. "We know how to treat a guest." Nannie opened a cupboard door. She pulled out a cake tin. She lifted the lid. "Ta-dah!" she cried.

On our cake plate sat something that looked sort of like a cake, but not really. It was lopsided. The top slanted down. It was covered with runny yellow icing. Nannie had decorated it, too. But the decorations were sliding down the sides of the cake.

"I hope you like peanut butter-lemon-fudge-butterscotch with raisins," said Nannie. She cut a slice of cake. Before she could serve it to Mr. Sand, though, it fell on the floor. "Oops!" cried Nannie. She picked it up, put it back on the plate, and handed it to Mr. Sand. "A little dirt never hurt anyone," she added.

I know my face turned red then. I was a member of a pig family. And I had lost my chance to go to Hawaii.

April Fool!

"Coffee, Mr. Sand?" asked Charlie. "Maybe that will help wash down the cake." (Mr. Sand had not tasted his slice of floor cake yet.)

"Coffee would be lovely," said Mr. Sand.

"Okay. The coffee-maker is on the counter. I'm sure you know how to use it. If we run out of coffee grounds, just add a little dirt from the garden. That is what we always do."

All right. I had had enough. "Charlie!" I

cried. "That is so rude! Mr. Sand is a guest! And a *judge*."

"Are you sure, Karen?" asked Charlie.

"Of course I am. I know a judge when I see one."

My big-house family was quiet for a moment. Then they yelled, "April Fool!" (Emily yelled, "Apra Foo!")

"April Fool?" I repeated.

"Yeah, we really got you!" cried David Michael.

"Honey, Mr. Sand is not a judge from the Beautiful Family contest. He is a friend of mine. We work together," said Elizabeth.

"You mean this was a joke?" I asked. I smiled. Then I laughed. "I do not believe it!" The rest of my family was laughing, too. Then I thought of something. "But I started the joke," I said. "How come you are finishing it? How did you find out about *my* joke?"

"We almost didn't find out," said Kristy. "We did not find out until this morning.

Sam answered the phone when Hannie called. He answered in the kitchen. You answered upstairs at the same time. And Sam sort of listened in. So he knew no judge was coming over."

"Yeah," said Sam. "Sorry for listening to your conversation, but I am glad I did. I told everyone else what you were doing. Then, while you were at Hannie's, we messed up the house. I know you think we are piggy sometimes. It was easy to fool you."

"You guys!" I cried.

"Well," said Daddy. "We better get to work. We have a big clean-up to do. Everyone clean up the mess you made. Karen, you help Emily."

Cleaning up was not easy. My family had made so *many* messes. But when we had finished, the house looked great.

"I bet we really *could* win a Beautiful Family contest now," I said. Then I looked at my watch. The afternoon was nearly over.

I was running out of time to play April Fool's Day tricks.

I sat at the kitchen table. I picked up the phone. I dialed a number. When someone answered, I said, "Hello, this is Brewer Repair Service. Is your refrigerator running? . . . It is? Then you better catch it!"

"Who is this?" asked my friend.

"It is Karen Brewer. April Fool! Hi, Gemma!"

"Karen? That was a good trick," said Gemma.

"Thank you. Wait until you hear the trick my family played on *me* today." I told Gemma about Mr. Sand and the moldy baloney and everything. I thought she would like the story. She did.

I was glad to have a new friend.

We had just hung up the phone when it rang again.

"Hello, Brewer and Thomas residence," I said.

"Hello. I am taking a survey. Is your refrigerator running?"

"Yes, it is," I replied. "So I better go catch it . . . Bobby!"

"Aw, darn," said Bobby Gianelli. "I *still* did not get you."

"And maybe you never will. Happy April Fools' Day, Bobby!"

"Happy April Fools' Day."

About the Author

ANN M. MARTIN lives in New York City and loves animals, especially cats. She has two cats of her own, Mouse and Rosie.

Other books by Ann M. Martin that you might enjoy are *Stage Fright; Me and Katie (the Pest)*; and the books in *The Baby-sitters Club* series.

Ann likes ice cream and *I Love Lucy*. And she has her own little sister, whose name is Jane.

Little Sister

Don't miss #28

KAREN'S TEA PARTY

"Who should we invite?" asked Nancy.

"Lets invite *all* the girls in our class," I said. "We want it to be a big, fancy tea party."

"Even Pamela?" asked Nancy.

"Yes. She thinks the boys are being dumb, too," I replied. "We will tell everyone to get really dressed up. Even dressier than we do for Mr. Peabody's School."

"Wow!" said Nancy.

"I will make brownies." (I decided I still loved to cook.) "I will cut them up small and put them on doilies. It will be perfect for lovely, lovely ladies," I said.

Little Sister™

by Ann M. Martin, author of *The Baby-sitters Club* ®

❑ MQ44300-3	#1	Karen's Witch	$2.75
❑ MQ44259-7	#2	Karen's Roller Skates	$2.75
❑ MQ44299-7	#3	Karen's Worst Day	$2.75
❑ MQ44264-3	#4	Karen's Kittycat Club	$2.75
❑ MQ44258-9	#5	Karen's School Picture	$2.75
❑ MQ44298-8	#6	Karen's Little Sister	$2.75
❑ MQ44257-0	#7	Karen's Birthday	$2.75
❑ MQ42670-2	#8	Karen's Haircut	$2.75
❑ MQ43652-X	#9	Karen's Sleepover	$2.75
❑ MQ43651-1	#10	Karen's Grandmothers	$2.75
❑ MQ43650-3	#11	Karen's Prize	$2.75
❑ MQ43649-X	#12	Karen's Ghost	$2.95
❑ MQ43648-1	#13	Karen's Surprise	$2.75
❑ MQ43646-5	#14	Karen's New Year	$2.75
❑ MQ43645-7	#15	Karen's in Love	$2.75
❑ MQ43644-9	#16	Karen's Goldfish	$2.75
❑ MQ43643-0	#17	Karen's Brothers	$2.75
❑ MQ43642-2	#18	Karen's Home-Run	$2.75
❑ MQ43641-4	#19	Karen's Good-Bye	$2.95
❑ MQ44823-4	#20	Karen's Carnival	$2.75
❑ MQ44824-2	#21	Karen's New Teacher	$2.95
❑ MQ44833-1	#22	Karen's Little Witch	$2.95
❑ MQ44832-3	#23	Karen's Doll	$2.95

More Titles... ➡